Studio Fun International
An imprint of Printers Row Publishing Group
A division of Readerlink Distribution Services, LLC
9717 Pacific Heights Blvd, San Diego, CA 92121
www.studiofun.com

Printers Row Publishing Group is a division of Readerlink Distribution Services, LLC.
Studio Fun International is a registered trademark of Readerlink Distribution Services, LLC.

All notations of errors or omissions should be addressed to Studio Fun International, Editorial Department, at the above address.

ISBN: 978-0-7944-5015-1
Manufactured, printed, and assembled in Dongguan, China.
First printing, May 2022. RRD/05/22
26 25 24 23 22   1 2 3 4 5

Disney · PIXAR

TOY STORY

studio **fun**

INTERNATIONAL

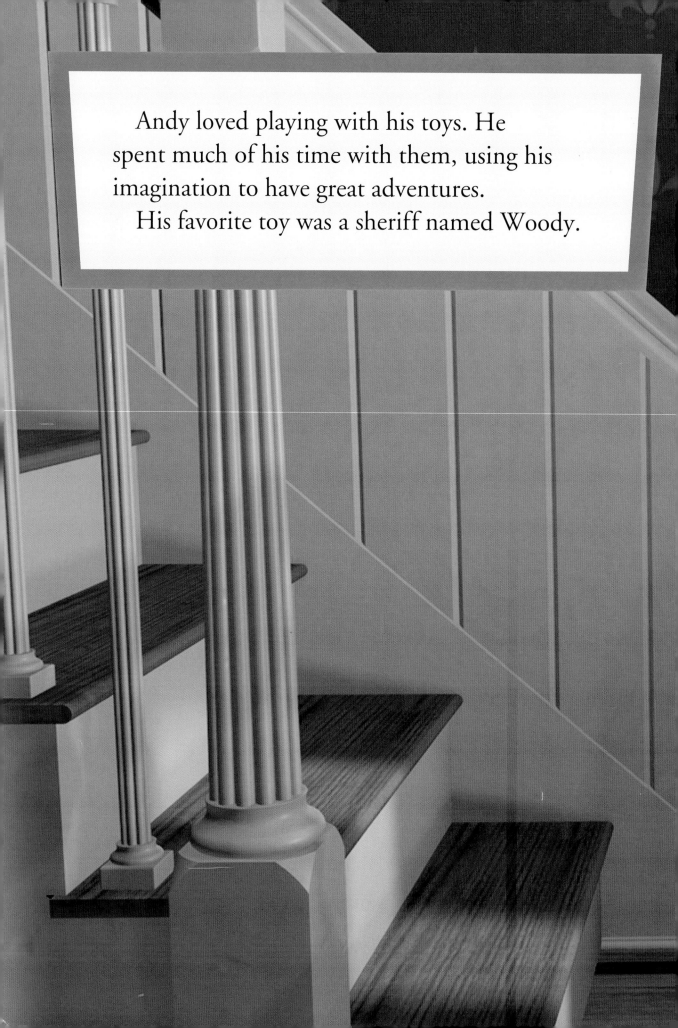

Andy loved playing with his toys. He spent much of his time with them, using his imagination to have great adventures.
His favorite toy was a sheriff named Woody.

Being Andy's favorite meant Woody was in charge of the other toys. He made sure they worked together to always be there for Andy.

One day, after Andy left the room and the coast was clear, Woody called the toys to a meeting. Andy's family would be moving soon and Woody wanted to make sure they were ready for the big day.

Woody also announced there had been a change in Andy's schedule. "Andy's birthday party's been moved to today," he explained.

The toys gasped. That meant Andy would be getting new toys sooner than expected! Many of them worried Andy might get a toy that he liked better than them. They were afraid of being replaced.

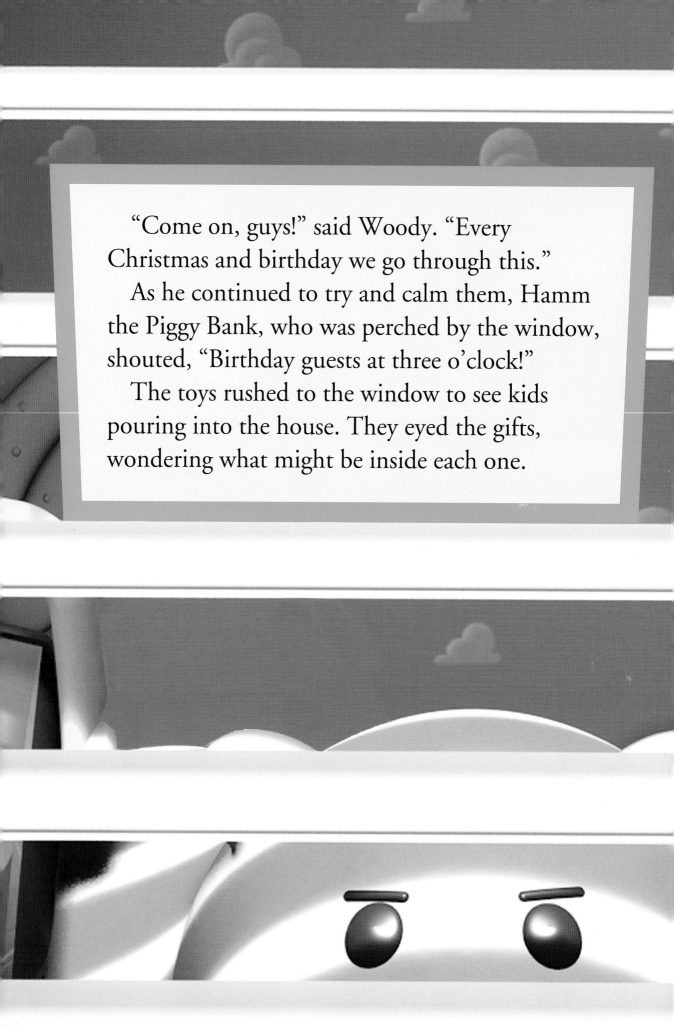

"Come on, guys!" said Woody. "Every Christmas and birthday we go through this."

As he continued to try and calm them, Hamm the Piggy Bank, who was perched by the window, shouted, "Birthday guests at three o'clock!"

The toys rushed to the window to see kids pouring into the house. They eyed the gifts, wondering what might be inside each one.

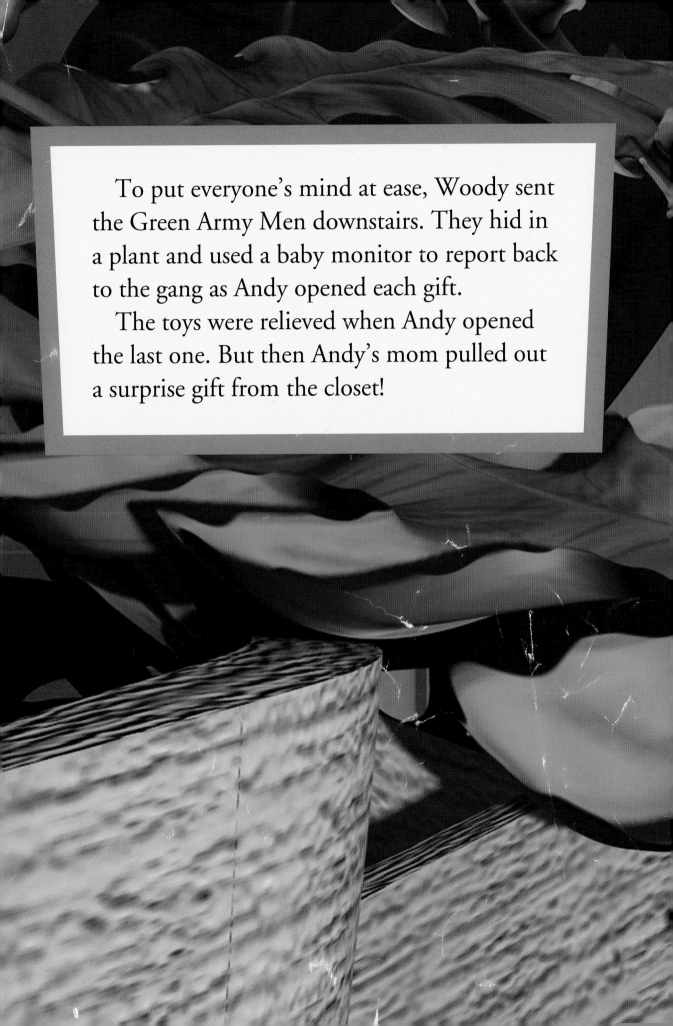

To put everyone's mind at ease, Woody sent the Green Army Men downstairs. They hid in a plant and used a baby monitor to report back to the gang as Andy opened each gift.

The toys were relieved when Andy opened the last one. But then Andy's mom pulled out a surprise gift from the closet!

Rex the dinosaur bumped into the monitor and the batteries fell out! Before they could fix it, they heard Andy and his friends barreling up the stairs! They quickly dropped into toy mode before the kids entered.

Andy put the new toy on his bed, knocking Woody to the floor!

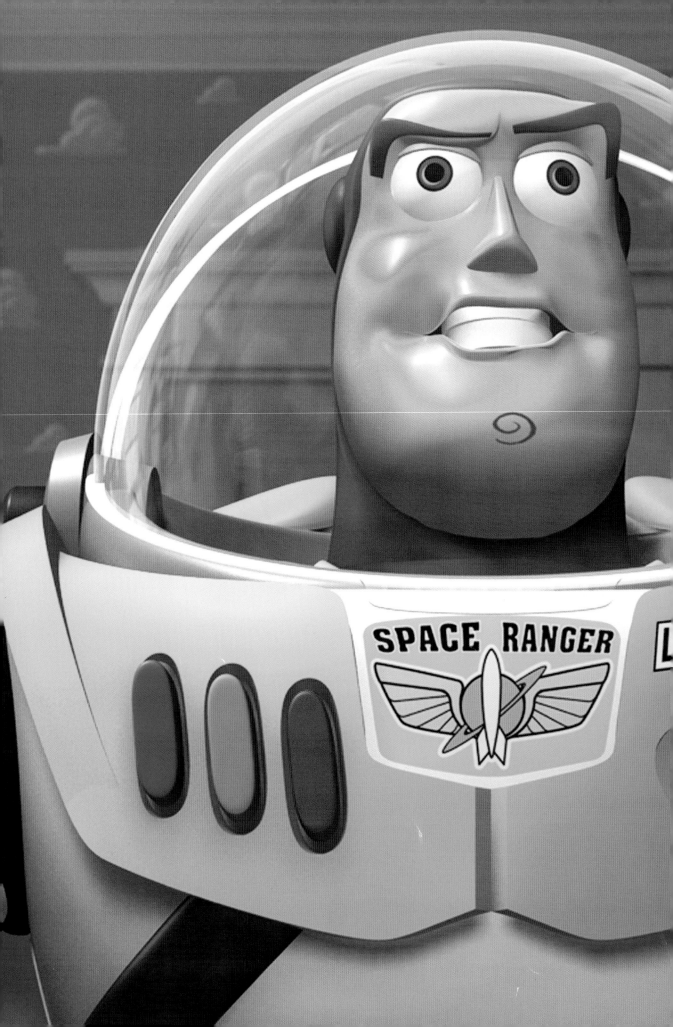

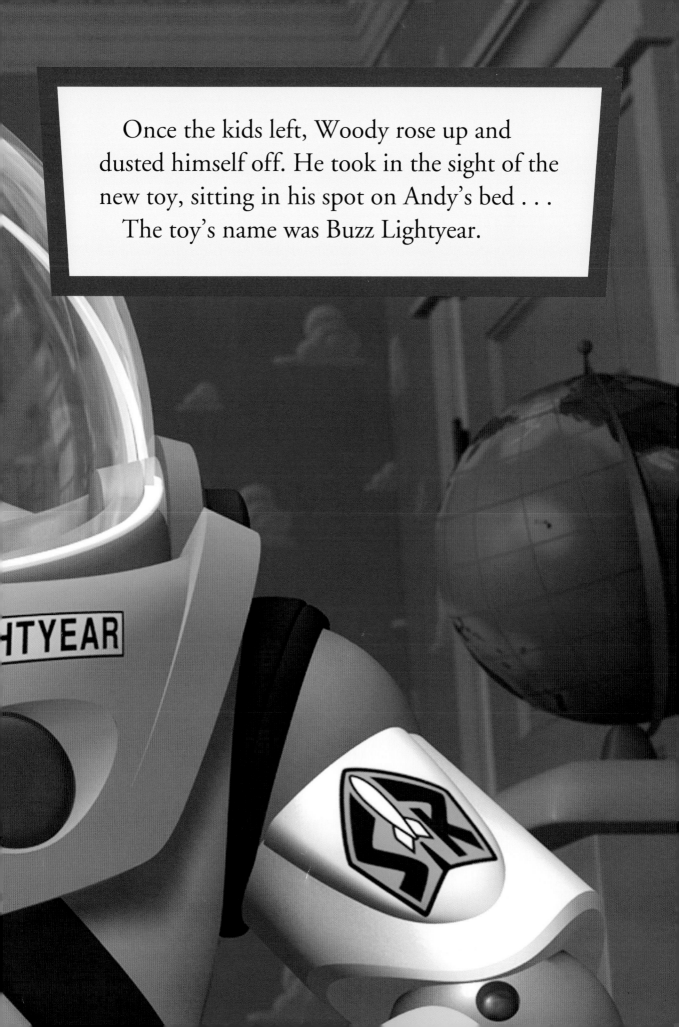

Once the kids left, Woody rose up and
dusted himself off. He took in the sight of the
new toy, sitting in his spot on Andy's bed . . .
The toy's name was Buzz Lightyear.

All the other toys were amazed by Buzz's
buttons and lights, but Woody was a little
annoyed. "All right, that's enough," he said.
"Look, we're all very impressed with Andy's
new toy—"

"Toy?" interrupted Buzz. He believed he
was a real Space Ranger, not a toy.

Woody laughed. "He's not a Space Ranger!
He doesn't fight evil or shoot lasers or fly—"

"Excuse me," said Buzz. He pushed a button on his chest and wings popped out on his back. The other toys gasped.

"Oh, impressive wingspan," said Hamm.

Woody scoffed. "These are plastic. He can't fly!"

"Yes, I can," said Buzz firmly. "Stand back, everyone!"

The toys parted as Buzz strutted to the bedpost and climbed up, determined to prove he could fly.

"To infinity and beyond!" said Buzz. Then he leapt off the bed!

Everyone watched in awe as he bounced off some toys and soared around Andy's room!

Buzz gracefully landed and everyone but Woody rushed toward him, cheering and clapping.

"That wasn't flying!" Woody said. "That was . . . falling with style."

But the others were too busy admiring Buzz to pay any attention to Woody.

As the days passed, Andy spent more and more
time playing with Buzz. Woody was beginning to
feel like he had been replaced.

One day, when Woody heard Andy's mom
say he could bring only one toy to Pizza Planet,
Woody wanted to make sure Andy chose him.

Woody sat in RC car and prepared to knock
Buzz off the bed to get him out of the way.

But instead, Buzz accidentally fell out the
bedroom window!

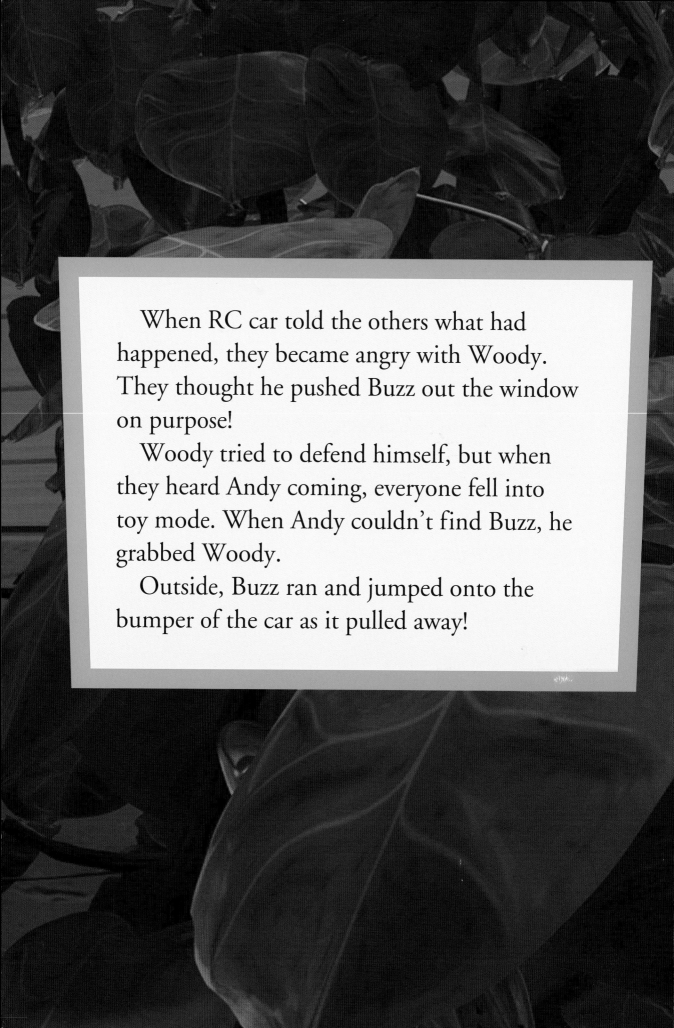

When RC car told the others what had happened, they became angry with Woody. They thought he pushed Buzz out the window on purpose!

Woody tried to defend himself, but when they heard Andy coming, everyone fell into toy mode. When Andy couldn't find Buzz, he grabbed Woody.

Outside, Buzz ran and jumped onto the bumper of the car as it pulled away!

On the way to the restaurant, Andy's mom stopped to get gas and Andy hopped out to help.

Buzz appeared and lunged at Woody. They wrestled and ended up falling out of the van! The two were so busy fighting that they didn't notice when the car pulled away.

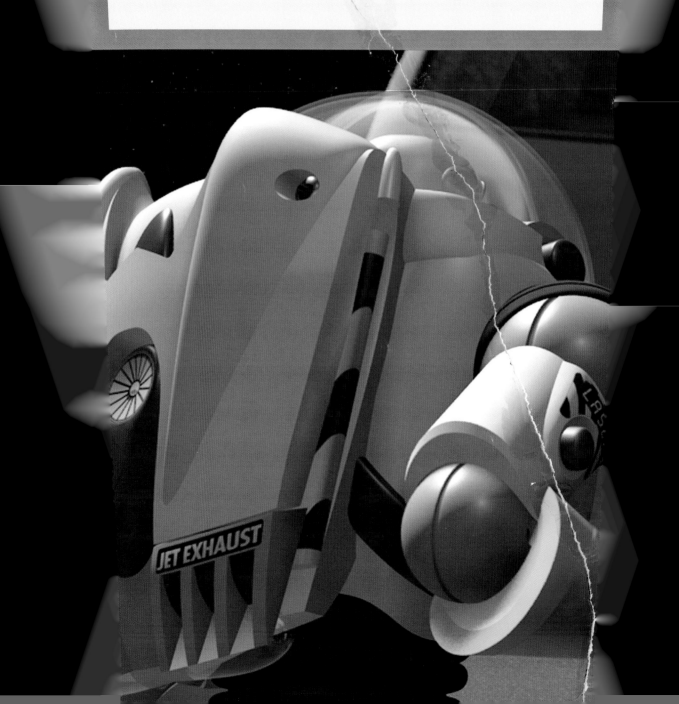

Buzz and Woody had no idea how they were going to get back to Andy.

Luckily, a Pizza Planet delivery truck pulled up. But Woody needed Buzz to come with him. Without Buzz, Woody would never be able to convince the other toys that it had all been one big misunderstanding.

After climbing into the truck, Woody and Buzz were on their way to Pizza Planet—and Andy!

After a wild ride through the city, they arrived at Pizza Planet.

Woody wanted to find Andy, but Buzz ended up inside a claw game with a group of toy aliens.

Woody tried to get Buzz out, but then a kid stepped up to play. They were trapped!

Woody couldn't believe it when he saw who was playing the game: Sid, Andy's mean neighbor who destroyed toys for fun.

Sid's face lit up with an evil grin as he lowered the claw, capturing both Woody and Buzz!

Sid took them home and locked them in his bedroom. When he stepped out, Woody and Buzz looked around to see a crowd of scary-looking toys. Sid had created them by taking the toys apart and combining them in different ways.

Woody knew they had to escape before Sid got to work on them!

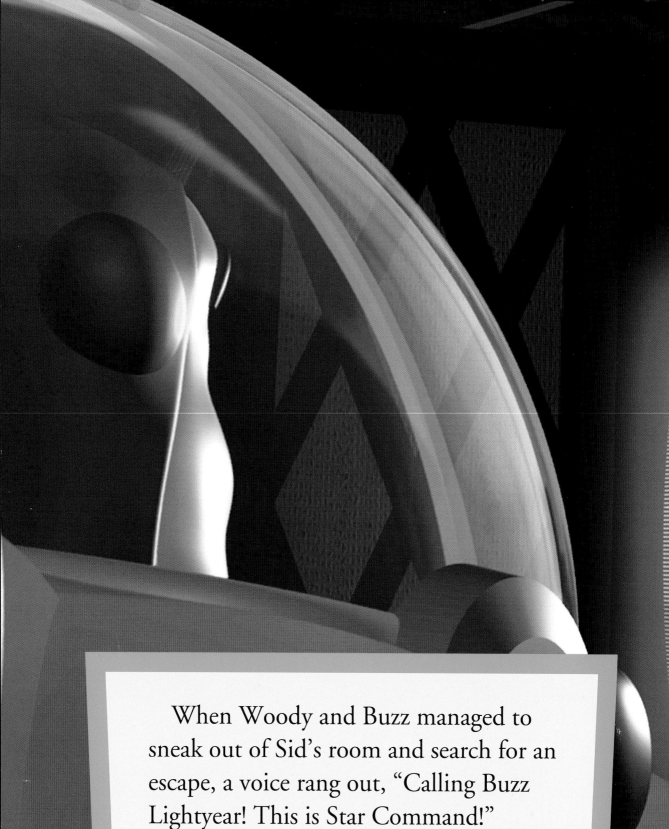

When Woody and Buzz managed to sneak out of Sid's room and search for an escape, a voice rang out, "Calling Buzz Lightyear! This is Star Command!"

Buzz eagerly followed the voice. Duty called! But he was shocked to see it was a television commercial.

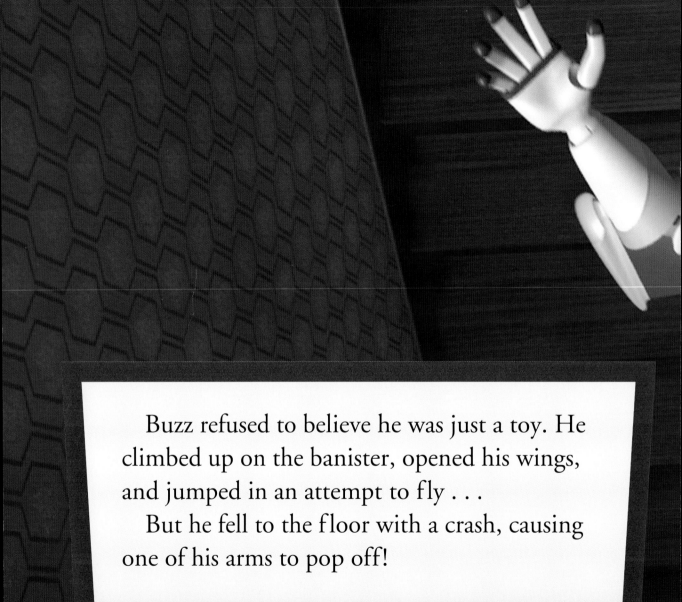

Buzz refused to believe he was just a toy. He climbed up on the banister, opened his wings, and jumped in an attempt to fly . . .

But he fell to the floor with a crash, causing one of his arms to pop off!

Later on, Sid's toys surrounded a terrified Buzz and Woody holding Buzz's arm. When the toys backed away, Woody and Buzz were surprised to see they had fixed Buzz's arm! It turned out the scary-looking toys were not scary at all.

"They fixed you!" said Woody.

That night, Woody tried to talk to Buzz, but he barely responded. He was sad that he wasn't a real Space Ranger. He didn't want to be a toy.

Woody explained how important being a toy was. "Look, over in that house is a kid who thinks you are the greatest, and it's not because you're a Space Ranger, pal. It's because you're a toy," said Woody. "You are his toy!"

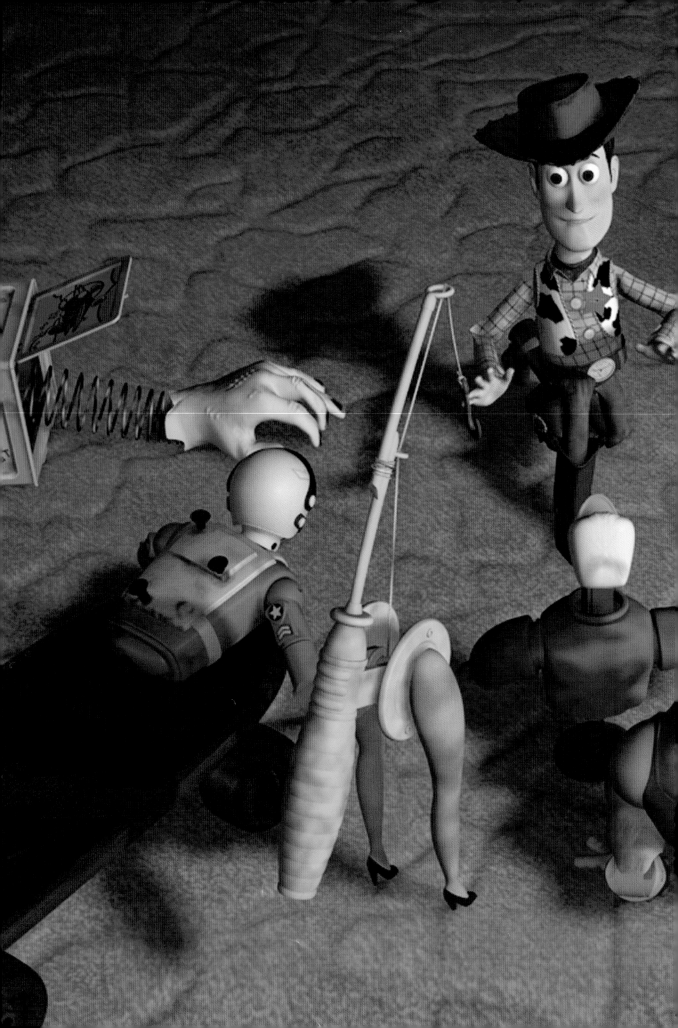

Woody's words inspired Buzz, and he wanted to get back home to Andy. But the next day, Sid grabbed Buzz and ran outside. He strapped a big rocket to him and was going to blow him up!

Woody came up with a plan. He and Sid's toys sneaked out to the backyard, determined to stop Sid and save Buzz.

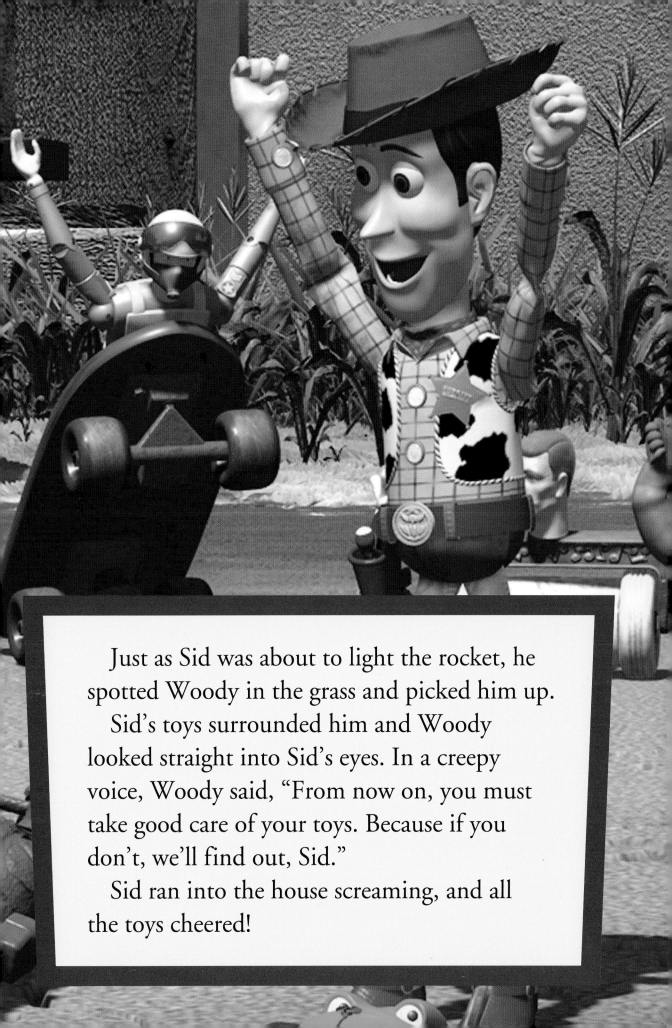

Just as Sid was about to light the rocket, he spotted Woody in the grass and picked him up.

Sid's toys surrounded him and Woody looked straight into Sid's eyes. In a creepy voice, Woody said, "From now on, you must take good care of your toys. Because if you don't, we'll find out, Sid."

Sid ran into the house screaming, and all the toys cheered!

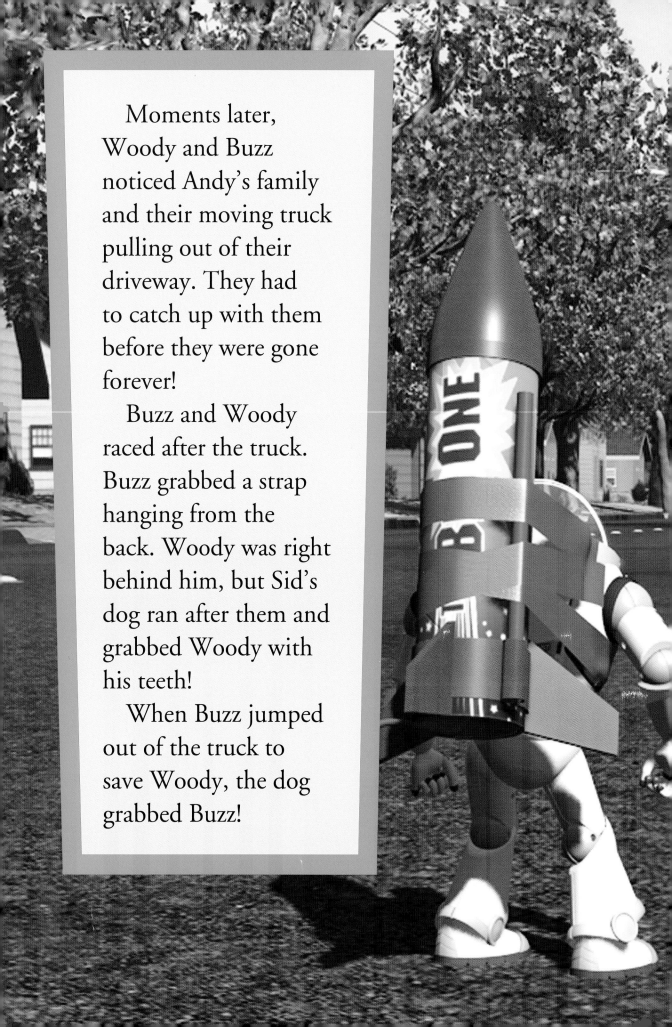

Moments later, Woody and Buzz noticed Andy's family and their moving truck pulling out of their driveway. They had to catch up with them before they were gone forever!

Buzz and Woody raced after the truck. Buzz grabbed a strap hanging from the back. Woody was right behind him, but Sid's dog ran after them and grabbed Woody with his teeth!

When Buzz jumped out of the truck to save Woody, the dog grabbed Buzz!

RC car darted out of the moving van to give Buzz and Woody a ride, and it looked like they were going to make it!

But then RC car's batteries ran out, causing them to skid to a stop.

Woody and Buzz almost gave up, until they realized they still had Sid's rocket. Woody lit the fuse and the two toys shot up into the air! They dropped RC car into the moving van, but Buzz held tight to Woody and the two kept going, higher and higher.

Buzz popped open his wings, releasing the rocket just as it exploded!

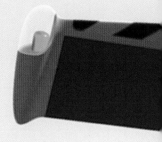

"Hey, Buzz! You're flying!" cheered Woody as they soared across the sky.

"This isn't flying," said Buzz. "This is falling—with style!"

Woody laughed. "To infinity and beyond!"

The two friends headed past the moving truck toward Andy's car.

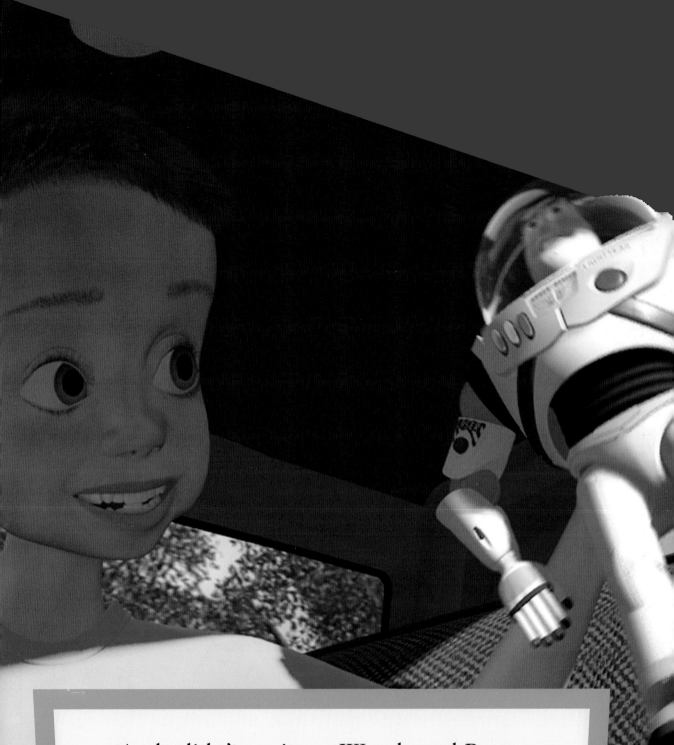

Andy didn't notice as Woody and Buzz slipped right through the sunroof, landing in the box beside him.

The friends had worked together to make it back to Andy—and nothing could be better than that.